Spaghetti and Peas

Gary Gautier

illustrated by Sheila Bailey

all about kids
publishing

San Jose

All About Kids Publishing, Inc.
6280 San Ignacio Avenue, Suite C
San Jose, CA 95119

Book Design by Shanti Nelson Design

Printed in Hong Kong

For information about permission to reproduce
any selection from this book write to:

All About Kids Publishing, Inc.
6280 San Ignacio Avenue, Suite C
San Jose, CA 95119

Library of Congress catalog card number: 000-111949
ISBN 0-9700863-6-9

My daddy was cooking
spaghetti and peas,
and chopping up onions
and garlic and cheese.

He sang while he cooked
with a "lolly-a-roo" and a
"do-be-do-wah,"
(and he whistles good too).

But I went to the yard
before Daddy was done,
singing is okay
but I wanted real fun.

I wanted adventures
and magical spells,
and frogs that were princes
and gold wishing wells.

And while I was thinking
I heard something stir,
and I saw something move
in a blink and a blur.

I spied through the turnips
and poked in the ground,
when something went "Pssst,"
and I slowly turned around.

Then I jumped a foot high
—when I saw what I did—
a snake in the lettuce
that squiggled and slid.

She came to a stop by
the stump of the tree,
flicking her tongue
and looking at me.

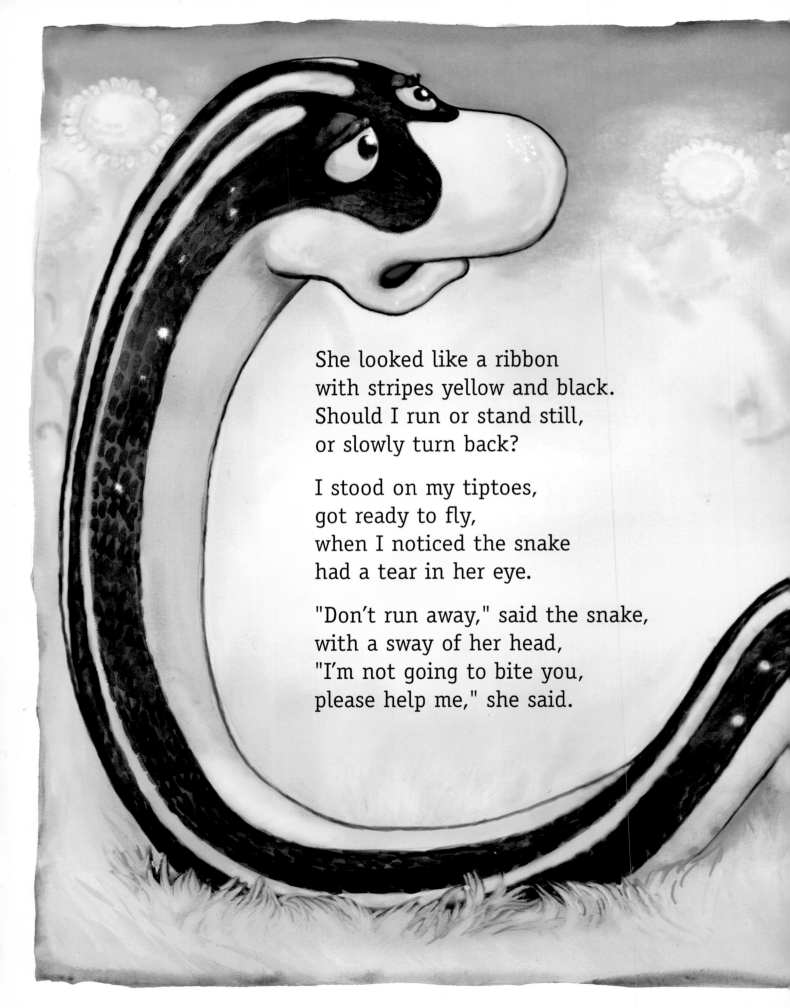

She looked like a ribbon
with stripes yellow and black.
Should I run or stand still,
or slowly turn back?

I stood on my tiptoes,
got ready to fly,
when I noticed the snake
had a tear in her eye.

"Don't run away," said the snake,
with a sway of her head,
"I'm not going to bite you,
please help me," she said.

"I saw a strange kitten run through the grass, and I hid in the garden waiting for it to pass.

"The kitten is now gone, but my babies are too. I'm afraid they are lost— what shall I do?"

"I'm Rachael," I told her,
"we'll find them, I bet."
"I'm Jane," said the snake,
"and I'm glad that we met."

We looked through the cabbage
and spinach and dill,
and all through the yard
and under the grill.

We ran past my dad
and opened my door,
and looked through my toys
that were covering the floor.

We looked in my lunchbox—
and then—what a sight!
All of Jane's babies
were snuggled up tight.

They were so thrilled
to get out of that box,
that they wrapped 'round my fingers.
and got in my socks.

They all kissed my cheeks
and my eyes and my chin,
and it tickled like feathers
all over my skin.

On our way to the yard
we ran right across
my daddy again
(he was cooking his sauce).

Marie from next door
heard the giggle and fuss,
and came right over
to play games with us.

We played with Jane's babies
up on the tree stump.
They were jumping like shoestrings,
(if shoestrings could jump).

They hid in my sandbox,
pretending to doze,
then we sank in our feet
and they squirmed through our toes.

Then Jane told her babies,
"Now kids, that's enough,
it's dinnertime, let's eat
some crickets and stuff."

Jane gave me a flickery
kiss on the cheek,
she was a little choked up,
but she managed to speak.

"We love you, Rachael,
you've been a true friend,
please come back and play
with my babies again."

Marie and I went inside
talking of snakes,
and when my dad heard us
he said, **"Goodness sakes!"**

"I hope you're not bitten
or frightened or hurt,
you'd better beware of
those snakes in the dirt."

"Oh no, Dad," I said,
"we were just having fun,"
and we told him all about
the things we had done.

He stood there amazed,
gave us each a big kiss,
and Marie and I finished
the story like this:

"Some snakes might bite
in the park or the woods,
but not Jane and her babies,
they love us for good."

Dad seemed to think
all of this was a bit odd.
He'd lift up his eyebrows
and now and then, he'd nod.

Then without saying a word
he gave us a squeeze,
and served us big plates
of spaghetti and peas.

The End